Dear Parent:
Your child's love of reading starts here!

Every child learns to read in a different way and at his or her own speed. You can help your young reader improve and become more confident by encouraging his or her own interests and abilities. You can also guide your child's spiritual development by reading stories with biblical values and Bible stories, like I Can Read! books published by Zonderkidz. From books your child reads with you to the first books he or she reads alone, there are I Can Read! books for every stage of reading:

SHARED READING
Basic language, word repetition, and whimsical illustrations, ideal for sharing with your emergent reader.

BEGINNING READING
Short sentences, familiar words, and simple concepts for children eager to read on their own.

READING WITH HELP
Engaging stories, longer sentences, and language play for developing readers.

READING ALONE
Complex plots, challenging vocabulary, and high-interest topics for the independent reader.

ADVANCED READING
Short paragraphs, chapters, and exciting themes for the perfect bridge to chapter books.

I Can Read! books have introduced children to the joy of reading since 1957. Featuring award-winning authors and illustrators and a fabulous cast of beloved characters, I Can Read! books set the standard for beginning readers.

A lifetime of discovery begins with the magical words **"I Can Read!"**

Visit www.icanread.com for information on enriching your child's reading experience. Visit www.zonderkidz.com for more Zonderkidz I Can Read! titles.

"The King will reply, 'Truly I tell you, whatever you
did for one of the least of these brothers and
sisters of mine, you did for me.'"
—Matthew 25:40

ZONDERKIDZ

The Berenstain Bears Brother Bear and the Kind Cub
Copyright © 2017 by Berenstain Publishing, Inc.
Illustrations © 2017 by Berenstain Publishing, Inc.

ISBN 978-0-310-76023-8

Requests for information should be addressed to:
Zonderkidz, 3900 Sparks Drive SE, Grand Rapids, Michigan 49546

All Scripture quotations, unless otherwise indicated, are taken from
The Holy Bible, New International Version®, NIV®. Copyright © 1973,
1978, 1984, 2011 by Biblica, Inc.® Used by permission of Zondervan. All
rights reserved worldwide. www.Zondervan.com. The "NIV" and "New
International Version" are trademarks registered in the United States
Patent and Trademark Office by Biblica, Inc.®

Zonderkidz is a trademark of Zondervan.

Editor: Annette Bourland
Design: Cindy Davis

Printed in China

17 18 19 20 21 22 23 24 25 26 /DSC/ 10 9 8 7 6 5 4 3 2 1

ZONDERkidz

I Can Read!

BEGINNING
READING
1

The Berenstain Bears

Brother Bear
and the
Kind Cub

Living Lights™
A Faith Story

by Stan & Jan Berenstain
with Mike Berenstain

Brother Bear liked to play sports.

He liked to draw.

He liked to fish and play games.

But the thing he liked to do most

was build model airplanes.

Brother Bear started making planes
with Papa when he was little.
Soon, Brother could build models
by himself.

And it was fun to watch them fly.

One day, Brother and Sister

went to the park.

Brother had his new plane.

Sister met her friends.

One girl had a brother named Billy.

Billy saw Brother's new plane.

He wanted to see it up close.

"Wow!" said Billy.

Brother got the plane ready.

He picked it up.

"May I help you fly it?" asked Billy.

Brother was careful with his airplanes.

But he remembered how Papa

let him help when he was little.

"Okay, you may help," said Brother.

Brother let Billy hold the model.

"Here we go," said Brother.

"One, two, three … fly!"

They let go.

The plane went up above the park.

Then it began to fall.

It hit the ground with a *crunch!*

Brother and Billy ran to the plane.

It was broken.

"Will you fix it?" asked Billy.

"Build them, fly them, crash them,
fix them!" said Brother.
"That's what I say."

"Could I help?" asked Billy.

"Billy, you are too young," said Billy's sister.

"That's okay," said Brother.

"I could use a little help."

Billy went to the Bears' tree house.

Mama and Papa were happy

Brother was being kind to Billy.

"The Bible says be kind," said Mama.
"The Bible also says
any kind thing you do will always
come back to you," said Papa.

Blessed are
the merciful,
for they will
be shown
mercy.
Matthew 5:7

Every day that week,
Billy helped Brother
with the plane.

He learned a lot and had fun.

Brother had fun too.

The next week, Brother and Billy

took the plane to the park.

Everyone came to watch.

Billy and Brother let it fly.

"This looks like a good flight!"

said Brother.

The plane flew on and on.

Finally it came down.

The plane landed across the park.

It was in perfect shape.

"Hurray!" yelled Billy.

Brother saw a group of older cubs

coming into the park.

Their coats said

"Bear Country Rocket Club."

They were setting up a model rocket!

"May I help launch the rocket?"
asked Brother.

"You are too young," they said.

Brother was sad.

Billy went to talk to one of the cubs.

"Billy says you let him help
with your plane," said the older cub.

"That was nice. You can help us too."

So Brother helped the rocket club.

They let him hold things and

move things around.

When it was time to fire the rocket,
they let Brother push the button!

"5, 4, 3, 2, 1 … *fire!*"
said the cub in charge.

There was a loud *WHOOSH!*

The rocket shot up into the sky.

The rocket drifted back to earth.

It was twisted and burned.

"Will you fix it?" asked Brother.

"Build them, fly them, crash them, fix them!" said the older cub.

"May I help?" asked Brother.

"Sure you can," said the older cub.

Because Brother was kind
to someone younger than himself,
he became the youngest cub
in the Bear Country Rocket Club.
And he was proud!